Mrs. Kolden's Class,

Many adventures!

by Ryan Jacobson
Illustrated by David Hemenway

11/08

Adventure Publications, Inc.
Cambridge, MN

## Dedication

For Donnie, who started me on my writing adventures.

## Acknowledgements

A very special thanks to Evelyn Hughes, whose input was invaluable. And thank you to my wife, Lora, for putting up with me on those endless nights in front of the computer screen.

Edited by Brett Ortler
Cover design by Jonathan Norberg

10 9 8 7 6 5 4 3 2 1

# TABLE OF CONTENTS

# HOW TO USE THIS BOOK

*Lost in the Wild* is a work of fiction. Many of the dangers presented are done so to create drama. For instance, Black Bears and Gray Wolves are shown as vicious animals. In real life, while you should be cautious of them, there is little reason to fear them. (See page 150 for more information about Black Bears and Gray Wolves.)

As you read this adventure, you'll sometimes be asked to jump to a distant page. Follow these instructions. You might also be asked to choose between two or three options. Decide which is best, and go to the corresponding page. But be careful. Some of the options will lead to disaster. Finally, if a page offers no instructions or choices, simply turn to the next page.

Remember, *this is just a story*. The book is not meant to take the place of professional advice and/or training. The publisher and author disclaim any liability for any loss or injury that may result from the use of the information.

Please, respect all wildlife and nature. Enjoy the story!

# PROLOGUE

You scan your memories, trying to remember what you read. How to survive a bear encounter. How to survive a bear encounter. How to survive a bear encounter.

The book was very specific, but the answer depends on the type of bear. Now your sister is face to face with a large, angry black bear. But what should you tell her? Run? Climb a tree? Stand her ground?

Everything depends on this decision. If you make a mistake, it could mean the difference between life and death. But you can't remember what to do, and you're running out of time.

**Turn to page 7.**

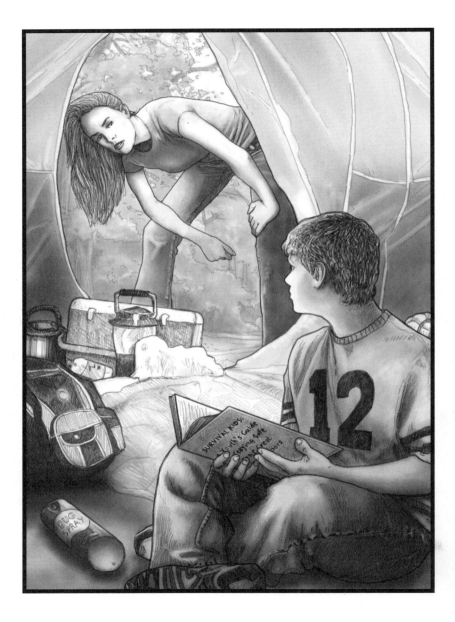

sound of your tent's entrance being unzipped. You look up to see your fourteen-year-old sister peeking through, her long, brunette hair a tangled mess.

"Are you *ever* coming out?" she asks.

"No," you snap.

Your family has shared some pretty terrible vacations: food poisoning in South Dakota's Badlands, car trouble in Kentucky's Appalachian Mountains and a flu outbreak on the way to New York City. But you have a feeling this trip is going to be the worst.

"Fine," says Kate. "See if I care." She backs out of the tent, disappearing from view.

"Zip it up," you shout after her. "You're letting all the bugs in!"

Next, it's your mom's turn. She calls from outside the tent. "Honey, I'd like you to come and join us for a while."

"Not until I know it's safe," you answer.

"You have nothing to worry about," says your dad. "Your mother and I are here to protect you."

"What about the mosquitoes? How will you protect me from them?"

Kate laughs, in her annoying, high-pitched squeal. "Mosquitoes? You're afraid of mosquitoes?"

# 1
## CAMPOUT

You remember the day your parents told you about the camping trip to Minnesota's Boundary Waters. You were so excited that you cleaned your bedroom, folded the laundry and even offered to organize the garage. You'd never been camping before, but your sister Kate is an outdoors nut. She made camping sound like a perfect vacation.

Unfortunately, you didn't know how hard it would be. You miss your video games and air conditioning, and let's not forget sleeping on a soft mattress.

Of course, Kate is having a great time, but why does she like it here? The air is thick with bugs, so thick that it makes the sunlight seem dampened and dull. The endless buzzing, stinging and itching really freak you out, so you retreat to your blue tent. You're safe inside, and you can almost forget about all of the wild creatures that prowl the forest.

As long as you're sitting there, you decide to read your new book, *Survival Kids: A Youth's Guide to Staying Safe in the Great Outdoors*. But you're soon interrupted by the

"That's enough, Kate," says your mother.

"It's not funny," you holler. "They could bite you and give you that virus, the one that makes people sick."

Outside, Kate whispers, "I think Jamie means West Nile." Then she adds loudly, "That's ridiculous. Your chances of getting sick from a mosquito are so small, I can't even calculate it. It's like a billion to one or something. Now come out. I want to go swimming."

What will you choose to do?

*You're afraid of the Great Outdoors, but reading your book makes you feel safer. Plus, if something bad happens, your book might better prepare you to handle it.*

*However, maybe Kate is right. There's probably nothing to fear. If you stay inside your tent, she's going to tease you for years. Besides, swimming sounds like fun. It's time to get out and enjoy your family vacation.*

**If you choose to stay in your tent and continue reading *Survival Kids*, turn to page 40.**

**If you choose to put away the book and go swimming, turn to page 35.**

You reach the clearing with the two rangers. Kate isn't there. She's disappeared.

"I don't understand," you tell them. "She was supposed to wait right here."

The taller ranger bends down and picks something off the ground. "What color is your sister's shirt?"

You try to remember. "Red, I think."

He holds up a torn piece of cloth. It's red.

Your heart fills with a sense of doom. "That looks like my sister's. Where is she? What happened?"

The ranger tries to comfort you. "Settle down, Jamie. It doesn't mean anything."

*Or maybe it means the bear came back and took her!* You're about to say so when the other ranger interrupts. "We have Jamie's dad on the radio. He's on his way here."

**Turn to page 24.**

The world around you is dark. You must have fallen asleep reading. But what awakened you?

As if answering your question, Kate whispers beside you. "Psst, Jamie . . . Jamie, wake up."

You rub the sleep from your eyes. "What time is it?"

"Almost four a.m.," she says.

That's way too early! You roll over, hoping to fall back asleep, but Kate grabs your arm and pulls you toward her. She clicks on a flashlight and shines it into your face. The pain is intense. You squint. You try swatting the light away. It doesn't help.

"Knock it off, Kate."

"Jamie, get up. I need your help."

**Turn to page 27.**

Despite the danger, you won't leave Kate behind. You fight against the waves, swimming in circles.

"Kate!"

Precious minutes pass. You're afraid you won't find her. You imagine the worst.

"Kate!"

What if her life jacket failed? What if she was knocked out? What if she doesn't make it?

"Kate!"

You fight forward. You swim faster. You thrash against the brutal storm.

"Kate!"

Then it happens. You thought it would come slowly. You thought you'd have time to react. You were wrong. Your rush of adrenaline wears off. You're out of energy.

You can't swim. You can't fight the waves. You can't even lift your arms. You're at the mercy of the storm.

The waves pound you, one after another. Without enough strength to turn away from them, you're overcome by the onslaught.

You choke on a mouthful of water. You gag and try to vomit. But before you can, the next wave crashes against you, forcing more water down your throat.

You can't breathe. You can't even gasp for air.

How long since you took your last breath? How much longer can you last?

The answer comes too quickly.

You think of Kate. You hope she's made it to safety. She probably has. Then everything fades to black, and it's the last thought you ever know.

**Turn to page 139.**

You roll your eyes. "I don't care what you say. I'm not going. You can't make me."

"Fine," says Kate. "See if I do anything for you *ever again*. And for your sake, you better hope nothing happens to me." She stomps out of the tent.

You feel a tinge of guilt. Did you do the right thing? Should you have gone with her? Will she be okay?

You fall asleep worrying.

**Turn to page 38.**

You stay in the clearing for a long time. You're afraid to talk. You're afraid to move. You're afraid to do anything that might attract the mama bear's attention.

Mosquitoes torment you. You watch as they land on your flesh, time and again. They suck your blood. You begin to itch. It's almost more than you can take.

Finally, your fear begins to fade. You fend off the cloud of mosquitoes, and you even manage a short nap.

When you wake up, you consider your options. You can search the area, in case the mama bear dropped your backpack nearby. Or you can return to the lake.

What will you choose to do?

*If you stay in the forest, you make it hard for rescuers to find you. At the lakeshore, you might get spotted by a passing boat.*

*However, you can't be sure that anyone will find you tonight. There are supplies in your backpack that might help you.*

**If you choose to go back to shore, turn to page 20.**
**If you choose to look for your bag, turn to page 44.**

***HINT: If earlier in the story you chose to stay in your tent and read, turn to page 144 for a helpful hint.***

The direction you chose is the right one. You're sure of it. You allow yourself another minute of rest then continue on your way.

The terrain becomes increasingly difficult. You crawl over boulders, squeeze between trees and cross through waist-deep streams.

The vegetation at your feet grows thick. You're forced to lift your foot above your knee just to take a step. To make matters worse, the terrain slopes upward, lifting you farther from the lake below.

Exhaustion sets in. You stop paying attention to where you're going.

You step forward, and the dirt beneath you gives way. You tumble downward into a deep hole, and you land with a thud.

For several minutes you find it hard to breathe, but that's the least of your worries. You're in a pit that's deeper than your basement. You can't see a way out. You're trapped.

You spend hours screaming for help. No one hears you.

The hours become days.

You're lost and alone. You finally admit that no one will ever find you. You'd cry if you had any tears left, but you used them up some time ago.

All you can do now is ask yourself what would have happened if you made a different choice on that fateful day?

**Turn to page 139.**

You stroll up the trail toward camp, and you laugh about the great time you had swimming. The cool lake water was a refreshing escape from this hot day. And who would've guessed that your sister could be so much fun?

But as the trail weaves up through the forest, your fears return. There could be a skunk, an owl or coyote around every bend.

When you reach your family's campsite, your mom and dad are cooking hot dogs by the fire. You devour a couple of blackened wieners. Then you hurry back inside your tent.

You're glad you shared that time with Kate, but you wonder if you would've been better off reading your book. Once you finish it, you won't have anything to worry about. You'll stay safe, no matter what happens.

Fortunately, there's still time to read a few pages before sunset. You flip open the book and begin a new chapter: "How to Survive a Bear Encounter."

**Turn to page 11.**

The thought of waiting in one spot all day makes you feel helpless, like you can't take care of yourself. Besides, Kate might need you, wherever she is. So you'll walk along the shoreline. Even if you don't find her, a passing boat might stop and offer some aid.

The morning sunlight burns the back of your neck, as you peel off your wet life jacket and toss it to the ground. Now, all that's left to decide is which direction to go.

What will you choose to do?

**If you choose to go left, turn to page 79.**
**If you choose to go right, turn to page 37.**

"Kate, we need to get moving" you tell your sister.

She doesn't answer.

"Kate, we need to go back to the shore. We'll have a better chance of being rescued."

Silence. You wait.

Finally, she speaks. "I'm not going anywhere. I'm staying here, where there aren't any bears."

"Kate, come on."

"No, Jamie. And I'm not talking about it any more."

*Now what?*

You know you should get to the waterfront, but you don't want to leave without Kate.

What will you choose to do?

*You're sure that, if you remain hidden from rescuers inside this forest, you won't be found before sunset. And you don't want to spend the night out in the open.*

*However, leaving Kate behind means both of you will be alone again. That puts each of you in greater danger. You're safer if you stay together.*

**If you choose to stay with Kate, turn to page 120.**
**If you choose to go alone, turn to page 66.**

Kate is helpless. You can't fight so many wolves. There is no option. You'll protect your sister no matter what, and the best way to do that is by leading the animals away.

"Hey, wolves," you shout. "I'm here! Come and get me!"

Then you run. As fast as you can. As long as you can.

"Follow me! I'm here! I'm right here!"

It doesn't work. Not one of them chases you. They're *all* still with your sister.

You need to get back. But which way did you come from? Which way should you go?

You see only trees and darkness. You're lost. Your sister needs you, and you can't do anything about it. You hope and pray that the wolves haven't found her.

"Kate!"

Does she hear you?

"Kate!"

Will she answer?

"Kate!"

*Can* she answer?

You collapse to the ground, sobbing.

There, you finally fall asleep.

**Turn to page 127.**

# 10
## HUNGRY

It's important to mark your trail as you go. Otherwise, you may not be able to find Kate when help arrives. You don't have any equipment, so you do the best thing you can think of: You break a tree branch every twenty steps.

You've been walking for hours. Your energy is low. You haven't eaten or had much to drink in more than a day. Your head is pulsing. You feel dizzy. Each step is harder to take than the last.

Your mind wanders. You're not paying attention. *You've stopped marking your path!*

Panic comes. Will you ever see Kate again?

You search for several minutes. The problem isn't that you *can't* find a broken branch. It's that you find too many. There are broken branches everywhere.

You discover too late that this isn't the best way to leave a trail. But all you can do is keep going.

You find what you hope is one of *your* broken branches, and you continue your mission. But you need to eat.

You move slowly, taking special care to mark the path. For Kate's sake, you're willing to eat anything. You'll even swallow a bug, if you can find one larger than a mosquito.

You hunt for several minutes. You don't capture an insect or a spider. Instead, you happen upon something better: a patch of mushrooms and wild berries. Your first instinct is to devour all of the food in sight, but you stop yourself. You remember that it's best to avoid eating *any* wild fruits and vegetables because many of them are poisonous.

In this case, it's a matter of life and death. You're willing to take the risk. But to be safe, you'll eat just one of the available foods.

The decision is dangerous. If you choose poorly, you'll get sick and possibly even die. But you have to eat something, or you'll soon be too weak to carry on.

**If you choose to eat mushrooms, turn to page 122.**
**If you choose to eat red berries, turn to page 68.**
**If you choose to eat white berries, turn to page 112.**

***HINT: If earlier in the story you chose to stay in your tent and read, turn to page 74 for a helpful hint.***

After that, your memories become hazy and blurred. You remember telling your dad what you know about Kate's whereabouts. You remember him guiding you toward your mother. And you remember him running off.

You remember traveling to a nearby ranger station. You remember crying as you try to explain what's happened. You remember the police and helicopters and search parties.

You remember the next day. And the next. And the next. They meld together into weeks.

You remember the weeks becoming months.

And you remember the day your dad tells you Kate is gone. She's never coming back.

Memories are all you have left of your sister—memories and a haunting question: What would've happened if you had made a different choice?

**Turn to page 139.**

After more than three hours of walking, you begin to lose hope. You should have found *something* by now. Where is the shore? You're tired, your body aches, and you want this nightmare to be over.

You force a path through cluster after cluster of trees. It's an exhausting process, but at last you push, past a final wave of leaves and branches, into a vast clearing.

The bright sun and cloudless sky blind you for a brief moment, and you don't immediately realize where you are. But then you see the beautiful, blue lake. Suddenly it makes sense. You've found your way out of the forest.

You rush into the cool water and splash around. Then, feeling as refreshed and as comfortable as possible, given the situation, you slump into the warm sand and wait.

**Turn to page 140.**

Before this vacation, you never would've been able to read a map. But yesterday, Kate spent part of the car ride showing you how. It almost made you glad that she's gone camping so many times with your cousins.

This morning, you put your new skills to the test. You followed the map to a secret fishing spot your dad had circled in red. (It's where your grandpa used to take him so many years ago.) You couldn't stop grinning after you led Kate straight to the place, using only the map and her compass watch. Of course, she pretended it was no big deal.

The bad news is that it's taken more than an hour of hard paddling to get here. According to the map, you're nearly three miles away from camp.

The sun begins to rise, shining brightly against the right side of your face, and you wonder why you needed to go so far. As if reading your mind, Kate answers. "Dad will think it's cool if we catch breakfast at his secret spot."

You're nervous about being on the water, but at least the fishing turns out to be good. As you reel in your first catch, you finally admit that you're having fun. Kate laughs and splashes you, and you continue pulling in fish.

**Turn to page 36.**

# 2
# SURPRISE

"What do you mean you need my help?" you ask.

"It's Mom and Dad's anniversary today," says Kate. "I want to do something special for them, but I can't do it without you."

You try to remember your older sister ever asking for *your* help before. You don't think she has. The surprise of her doing so is enough to jolt you awake. You sit up in your sleeping bag, feeling important. "What do you need from me?"

"Mom and Dad are still asleep. We can sneak out and catch some fish. Then we'll—"

"No way," you interrupt. "It's too dangerous. I'm staying right here."

"It's their anniversary. Think about all the nice things they do for us. They deserve this."

You shake your head. "My book says that, when you're camping in the woods, you should never go anywhere without telling an adult first."

"Oh, forget your stupid book," says Kate. "This is really important." She pauses, then adds, "Please? I'll take your turn washing dishes for a week."

"But Kate, I don't . . . I can't . . . Just go without me."

"I will if I have to, but I'm not good at canoeing alone. You know that."

You laugh so loudly that Kate hushes you. "You're right," you tell her. "Without me, you'd probably end up paddling around in circles."

She ignores your teasing. "What if I go and something happens to me? How would *that* make you feel?"

"I wouldn't care. It was *your* idea," you answer gruffly.

Kate smiles. "You'd be haunted by guilt." She punches your arm playfully. "Come on. You know I'm good at the fishing part. We won't be gone long."

What will you choose to do?

*Before now, Kate has never asked for your help. She wouldn't do so unless she really needed you. And what if something goes wrong? What if she gets hurt or worse? Would you ever be able to forgive yourself if you weren't there to save her?*

*However, this sounds like a dangerous plan. You're safe and sound, right where you are. If you go with your sister, who*

knows what kind of trouble you'll encounter? And what if something bad happens to both of you? No one will be there to rescue either of you.

**If you choose to help Kate catch fish for your parents, turn to page 42.**

**If you choose to stay in your tent and go back to sleep, turn to page 14.**

It isn't long before the journey wears you down. You've been walking through water, over rocks and around trees for hours. You haven't seen or heard anyone. You're hungry and you're thirsty.

You consider taking a drink from the lake, but you can't remember if lake water is safe. You don't have your book to double-check, so for now you decide to wait. You can always drink the water later.

Doubt creeps into your mind. Were you wrong about the sun? Are you moving farther away from help? What if you're walking into a deserted area and no one *ever* finds you?

You stop. You take a moment to think.

Should you continue forward? Should you wait where you are? Or should you turn around and go back?

What will you choose to do?

**If you choose to keep walking in the same direction, turn to page 41.**

**If you choose to stop and wait, turn to page 48.**

**If you choose to go back, turn to page 97.**

# 6
# FACE-OFF

"Don't move," you order. "Stay there. Pretend you're not scared!"

It sounds crazy, but it's Kate's only hope. If she can stand still, without flinching, the bear might see her as a threat and think twice about attacking.

Every stride brings the large animal closer. But to Kate's credit, she does as you tell her. She doesn't budge. Instead, she raises her arms and growls.

For a second you fear the worst. The bear won't stop. She'll maul your sister. But then, just three feet away, the mama bear ends her charge. You can hardly believe that anything moving so fast can stop so quickly.

The bear doesn't retreat. She studies Kate, nose twitching, as if waiting for your sister to make another mistake.

You hold your breath. Kate stands rigid like a statue. Will the bear leave her alone?

Finally, after several tense moments, the beast stands down. She casually lumbers away, grunting an order to her

cub, who never seemed to notice your presence or Kate's. The young critter trots alongside his mama, and the two step into the thick forest at the far end of the clearing.

The mama bear pauses. She looks back toward Kate then trudges to your backpack. She scoops up your bag in her teeth and glares at you, almost daring you to stop her. Then the animal follows her cub, disappearing with your backpack into the thick formation of trees.

Kate lets out a long, deep sigh, which turns into a loud, wild moan. Suddenly she's sobbing. Her body shakes. She collapses to the ground, folding herself into a tight ball.

You move to your sister and sit beside her. You wrap your arms around her and squeeze, mixing your own tears with hers. You're still scared, yes, but the two of you are together. And safe.

**Turn to page 15.**

"You're right," you admit. "I'm being silly. Let's do it. Let's go swimming."

"All right!" she exclaims. "I'll go and get my swimsuit."

You smile and tell her, "Don't walk down to the lake without me."

**Turn to page 18.**

It's another forty-five minutes before you notice that the wind has picked up and has pushed the canoe even farther from your campsite. You hear a loud rumble, and you look upward. Enormous black storm clouds roll toward you, blotting out the sunlight.

You barely have time to register the danger before the downpour begins.

**Turn to page 49.**

Without your map and compass, you don't know which way to go. But if you walk along the shore far enough, you're bound to find someone sooner or later.

With this in mind, you decide to go right. You turn and begin your long hike to safety.

**Turn to page 65.**

You're awake. You hear a thousand fingers tapping on a table. It's rain. No. Not just rain. A downpour.

Thunder booms. The tent shakes. You feel unprotected, but at least you're dry.

*Kate.*

Your eyes widen.

You rush outside, into the blazing storm.

"Kate!"

Did she decide to stay?

"Kate!"

Is she back already?

She doesn't answer.

Instead, your father emerges from his tent. "Jamie, what are you doing? Get back inside. It's not safe out here."

"Kate," you mutter. "She's gone."

**Turn to page 24.**

"Run," you tell her. "Get away!"

She turns and dashes toward the trees.

Kate's fast. The animal is faster. Four bounds and the bear tackles your sister.

She screams. You rush to her aid. It's the last mistake you ever make.

The bear turns to you. She lunges with a snarl. You see a flash of white teeth.

You have a moment to wonder what would've happened if you made a different choice. Then everything goes black.

**Turn to page 139.**

"I don't care," you tell your sister. "I'm staying right here. Go swimming by yourself!" You turn your attention back to your book, trying to block out the sound of your parents talking. It isn't easy to do.

"You never should've gotten that book, Jason," says your mom. "It has Jamie scared to death."

"I thought it would be comforting," your dad answers, defensively. "You know how Jamie's always worried about getting hurt."

You're happy your dad gave you the book. Once you read it, you won't have anything to worry about. You'll know what to do, no matter what.

You flip to the next page and begin a new chapter: "How to Survive a Bear Encounter."

**Turn to page 11.**

You chose the right direction. You're sure of it. You allow yourself another minute of rest, then continue on your way.

You come across a familiar trail. You recognize a pattern of trees. You arrive at your camp's beach—where Kate had invited you to swim. You've done it! You're back!

Excited and relieved, you dash up the hill, toward your family's campsite.

**Turn to page 82.**

You sigh, admitting defeat. "All right, fine. I'll go."

"Thank you!" Kate leans forward and squeezes your hand. "Let's get moving. I want to be back before Mom and Dad wake up. And remember to be quiet for a change."

Kate is always telling you what to do—and most of the time, not very nicely, even when you're helping. You glare at her. "I'm not doing this for you, you know. I'm doing it for Mom and Dad."

"So am I," she says, snidely. "Do you think I *want* you tagging along?"

"Good, then I'll stay here." You lie back down.

"No way! You already promised to come."

Sitting up, you snatch your blue backpack and begin stuffing it with supplies: a map, a flashlight and your book. "You don't always have to be so mean."

"You started it." But then Kate smiles. "I tell you what. I'll try to be nice, just for today."

You don't exactly believe her, but reluctantly, you agree to do the same.

"When you're all packed," she tells you, "grab some snacks from the bear bag. That's the bag in the tree down the path. We keep our food there so the bears can't reach it."

"I *know* what a bear bag is."

"Right, sorry. I'll get the fishing gear and life jackets."

She creeps away, leaving you to finish gathering your things. But if she wants you to pack food, you won't have room for everything else you might need. In fact, with the map, the flashlight, your book and the food, you only have room for four more things.

What will you choose to bring?

**To pick four items, turn to page 146.**

The bears should be long gone by now. You make sure Kate will be all right for a few minutes. Then you carefully walk toward the far end of the clearing.

Halfway there, you discover your mistake. The mama bear leaps out of the forest and barrels toward you. She must have been watching, in case you followed.

Kate shrieks. You don't have time to scream.

The giant animal launches herself onto you, forcing you to the ground.

You see a flash of white teeth. For a moment, you wonder what would've happened if you made a different choice. Then everything goes black.

**Turn to page 139.**

"Don't run," you tell her softly. "It'll chase. If it catches you . . ." You don't finish your sentence. You're afraid to say the words.

"Then what do I *do*?" Kate cries. "How do I get away?"

"Just do what I do," you say, making your voice as steady as possible. "And no matter what happens, no matter what the bear does, don't turn your back, and don't run."

You tilt your head downward, staring at the mama bear's paws. You take special care not to look her in the eyes. You begin talking slowly and calmly. "It's okay, bear. We're not going to hurt you. We're going to back up and leave you alone. We're going into the forest. You'll never see us again."

You continue talking in a low, monotone voice. You carefully take one step back. Then another. Then another. The distance between you and the bear grows.

Kate copies your every move. She mumbles quietly and begins moving backward.

"Good job, Kate," you whisper. "That's exactly right."

You take a final step, and you're safely within the cluster of trees. Kate is almost there too. She's just a few feet from the forest's shelter. You both relax, as you feel the danger fading. Kate even lets out a quick, sharp giggle of relief.

It's a tremendous mistake.

The sound startles the bear. Dropping onto all four legs, she charges toward your sister, snarling all the while.

Kate screams. "What do I do?"

You have to try something else. You have to decide fast. What will you choose to tell your sister?

**If you'll tell Kate to run, turn to page 39.**

**If you'll tell Kate to climb a tree, turn to page 117.**

**If you'll tell Kate to stand still, turn to page 32.**

You're tired. You're not sure you're walking in the right direction. But you're not sure you're walking in the wrong direction either. The best thing to do is sit down and wait. After all, Kate is alive. She *has* to be. And if she is, she's looking for you. You'll trust her to find you.

Besides, by now your mom and dad know that you're missing and that the canoe is gone. They'll come looking for you. You'll be with them again in a matter of hours.

You find a comfortable spot, you try to relax, and you wait for your rescuer.

**Turn to page 80.**

# 3
# THUNDERSTORM

You've never seen such heavy rain before. It pours onto you with such force that you can hardly see Kate sitting in front of you.

Thunder booms, rattling your bones. You feel a sudden terror. You remember the book's advice: "Never go anywhere without telling an adult," and you moan. The canoe is in the middle of an unknown lake, you can no longer see the shore, and your parents don't know where you are.

A bolt of lightning brightens the gray sky. Jagged streaks of light work toward the ground. Your situation has just gotten worse. You squeak like a frightened mouse as you imagine yourself being electrocuted.

Fear rises within you.

You need to move. You need to get away.

Panic sets in.

You do the worst thing possible: You stand up.

"We have to get off the lake! That lightning, it could kill us!"

"Jamie, sit down," shouts your sister. "Please! You're rocking the boat!"

You know she's right. You should sit. But you're no longer in control of your body.

"We have to do something! We have to—"

Your world is turned upside down. Your lungs burn. You choke down a mouthful of water.

The boat has rolled over. You're in the lake, and so is your sister.

You notice Kate's compass watch sink beside you. You're helpless. You don't know what to do. You're going to drown. You're sure of it.

But then you feel the tug of your life jacket. It pulls you upward. Thank God you're wearing it. You break the water's surface. You're alive!

You gasp for air, but you choke once again, as wave after wave slaps your face.

You take a deep breath and shout, "Kate!" You receive yet another mouthful of lake.

You listen for her reply but are answered only by the roars of water and wind.

You can't see her. You can't hear her. And you've lost sight of the canoe, as well.

Lightning flashes above you, but you continue your frantic search. Kate is bossy, and she gets on your nerves, but you don't want to lose her. This is all your fault!

For several long minutes you search the murky water. Your arms and legs grow tired. You won't last much longer. The lightning is getting closer, too. If it strikes anywhere nearby, you'll be a goner.

You should swim to shore, or you might never make it. But you don't want to leave Kate behind.

What will you choose to do?

*Kate is in the water somewhere, and you don't want to swim to shore without her. She might need your help. She might be drowning.*

*However, it will be difficult and perhaps impossible to find her in this storm. The lightning is getting dangerously close, and you're growing more tired every second.*

**If you choose to continue searching, turn to page 12.**
**If you choose to swim to shore, turn to page 83.**

"Jamie," says Kate, "we've been through a lot. I know I can trust you. You should get help. You have to make sure we get out of this alive."

**If you choose to search for help, turn to page 96.**
**If you choose to stay with Kate, turn to page 137.**

Your book said that, if you're lost and someone is looking for you, the best thing to do is wait in one spot. Kate is alive. She *has* to be. And if she is, she's definitely searching for you. You'll trust her to find you.

Besides, by now your mom and dad know that you and Kate are missing. The canoe is gone. They'll come looking for you. You'll be with them again in a matter of hours. You're sure of it.

You peel off your life jacket and toss it to the ground. It makes an excellent cushion.

**Turn to page 85.**

# 11
## DEN

There's only one choice: wait. Sooner or later, that mama bear will leave. When she does, you'll have a chance to reclaim the backpack.

It's hard to stand still, though. Every passing minute means Kate is still on her own. But you must be patient. When you retrieve the map, you'll be able to find your way out of the forest and get help for your sister more quickly. So you remain hidden.

It's more than an hour before the bear cub begins to roam. You silently watch as he trots away, and you pray that the mama bear will follow. But she doesn't budge.

For a moment, you fear that she'll let the cub wander alone. The grown bear will stay beside her den, guarding that backpack forever. But finally she pushes herself off the ground, yawns and reluctantly stalks after the young one.

Your opportunity has arrived. You wait for another five minutes, just to ensure that the bears are gone. Then you carefully creep toward the den.

With every step, you nervously glance in the animals' direction. If that mama bear catches you again, you're not sure what the beast will do. The thought is terrifying, and you try to block it from your mind. After all, it doesn't help to think about what might happen. But unfortunately, your sense of dread grows with every inch of progress.

The den is just a few feet away when you're suddenly overwhelmed with panic. You become certain that the ferocious bear is behind you, growling and ready to attack. You almost scream as you turn and peek backward, but neither the cub nor his mother is anywhere in sight.

Your brain tells you to move cautiously, but your body won't listen. Once again, fright gets the better of you. As quickly as you can, you dart the final few feet and dive into the bears' den, landing with a thud and a cloud of dirt.

You quickly scramble to your knees and dust yourself off. You try to stand, but you hit your head. The ceiling is low. In fact, the entire cave is smaller than you expected. It isn't much wider than your bedroom at home.

The den is dark and dirty, but you don't lose sight of your bag. You continue moving toward it, crawling inch by inch, until the bag is finally in your grasp. You feel a surge of excitement as you capture the prize.

The sensation doesn't last. The backpack has been torn open. Some of your belongings are missing.

If the map is gone, this entire ordeal will have been for nothing.

You frantically dig into the bag, holding your breath. The food has been eaten, but a closer inspection reveals that your other supplies (including the map) are still there.

You breathe a sigh of relief. You fold the bag in half and clasp it between your hands. But as you turn to leave, the den goes dark. Something *very* big is blocking the entrance. That can mean only one thing.

A loud, terrifying roar confirms your greatest fear. The mama bear is back!

You don't have time to move before a large, piercing jaw clamps onto your left foot. You expect a rush of pain, but it doesn't come. The bear has missed your skin. She's torn into the sole of your boot.

You try to pull away. The mama bear refuses to let go. She uses her powerful jaw to drag you closer. In moments, she'll release your boot and sink her teeth into your calf or thigh. If that happens, you'll *never* get away.

You remember the backpack. Maybe one of your tools will help you get free.

You reach into the bag. You slip your hand past the book and the map. You fumble for the right item. You pray that you'll find it in time.

**If you have pepper spray in your backpack, turn to page 136.**

**If you didn't bring pepper spray but have a pocket-knife in your backpack, turn to page 84.**

**If you packed neither, turn to page 90.**

Kate has been through too much already. You'll need her at full strength in the morning. Besides, the sounds are probably your imagination. There's nothing out there. It's best to let her sleep.

A few feet away, something growls.

You roll over.

You shake your sister. You're frantic.

Kate slowly opens her eyes. She's confused and groggy.

"Kate, there's something there."

Still half asleep, she looks at you, confused. "What are you—?"

A wild animal pounces on top of you. It's followed by second and then a third.

You hear the snarls and growls of wolves. They attack. You're helpless to defend yourself.

You see a flash of white teeth. You have a moment to wonder what would've happened if you made a different choice. Then everything goes black.

**Turn to page 139.**

You're scared. You don't know what to do. But then you realize the answer.

The leader is the key. His followers won't act until he does. You don't need to scare all of the wolves. Just the leader. If he runs, his pack will run too.

Kate moans again. You quickly hush her. You don't mean to be rude, but your *lives* are at stake.

You glance to the ground. A few sticks and rocks are within reach. Slowly, calmly, you bend down and wrap your fingers around the biggest stone; it's nearly the size of a baseball. With your other hand, you grab a stick, similar in length to a kitchen spatula.

So far, the wolves have been cautious. Their leader is probably sizing you up, wondering if you're worth the risk. Your only hope is to convince him that you're too much trouble to eat.

You launch the stone at the large wolf. He's an easy target, less than ten feet away. The rock hits him on his nose. He jumps back with a yelp.

You don't allow yourself to celebrate your perfect pitch. Instead, you continue your assault. You hurl the stick at the beast, followed by everything you can get your hands on: another stick, a small pebble, a rock, even your boots.

You don't dare move from your spot. The wolf might think you're retreating. You don't want to give him an excuse to attack.

You throw everything you've got. You miss him far more than you hit him, and you expect the creature to see through your act.

He cringes and ducks, but he doesn't charge.

Just as you're running out of ammunition, the wolf makes his decision. He barks at his followers. You prepare for the onslaught, grabbing a tennis-racket-sized stick you've been saving. But the wolves don't rush you. Instead, their leader turns away, tongue lolling. His pack waits for him to leave, and then each in turn follows.

You've done it! You've encountered an angry bear and a hungry pack of wolves, and you've survived both. But as you begin to congratulate yourself, Kate moans again.

You sit beside your sister and take her hand. She feels cold and sweaty to the touch. Her breathing isn't normal. It's quick and shallow.

"We're safe," you tell her. "The wolves are gone. I scared them away."

She smiles weakly, but when she looks at you, it's as if she's miles away. "Thanks, Jamie. Go ask Mom when the hot dogs will be ready."

You haven't had much first-aid training, but you've learned enough in swimming lessons to recognize the signs: clammy skin, rapid breathing and confusion. You check Kate's pulse. Her heart is pumping too hard and too fast. That confirms it. Your sister is in shock.

If you were anywhere else, you'd call an ambulance, but out here you don't have that option. If Kate is going to survive, it's up to you, and you have to do something fast.

What will you choose to do?

**If you choose to elevate her uninjured leg and keep her warm, turn to page 132.**

**If you choose to elevate her head and find her a drink of water, turn to page 118.**

*HINT: If earlier in the story you chose to swim with Kate, turn to page 143 for a helpful hint.*

Your muscles ache. Each minute lasts an eternity. How long have you been in the water? An hour? Two? You can't be certain, yet the rain hasn't even slowed.

You need to stop swimming. You need to rest. You can't go on, not any more. You roll onto your back, prepared to float wherever the waves might take you. But a flash of lightning reveals tree branches reaching out above you.

You flip onto your stomach again and notice a sliver of beach. Land is just a few feet ahead!

Your strength is renewed, if only for an instant. You pedal your legs with all of your might. You drive yourself forward, refusing to stop until your knees scrape a mixture of sand and rock beneath you.

You've made it.

You crawl out of the lake safely, onto solid land. You glance backward, hoping to see Kate coming out of the water behind you. But no one else is there.

More tired than you've ever felt before, you collapse into the mud and grass that surrounds the beach. You close your eyes and rest your head. Your last thoughts are again of Kate, as you fall fast asleep.

**Turn to page 101.**

It isn't long before the journey wears you down. You've been walking through water, over rocks and around trees for hours. You haven't seen or heard anyone. You're hungry and you're thirsty.

You consider taking a drink from the lake, but you can't remember if lake water is safe. You don't have your book to double-check, so for now you decide to wait. You can always drink the water later.

Doubt creeps into your mind. Are you walking in the right direction? Are you moving farther away from help? What if you're walking into a deserted area and no one *ever* finds you?

You stop. You take a moment to think.

Should you continue forward? Should you wait where you are? Or should you turn around and go back?

What will you choose to do?

**If you choose to keep walking in the same direction, turn to page 16.**

**If you choose to stop and wait, turn to page 48.**

**If you choose to go back, turn to page 97.**

"Okay," you tell her. "You stay here. I'll walk back to shore and see if I can get some help."

You wait for a couple of minutes, hoping she'll change her mind. She doesn't. So you make the difficult trek back to the lake alone.

**Turn to page 114.**

Your search is a disaster. It takes more than an hour of wandering before you come across a small creek, trickling through the woods.

You're too thirsty to resist. You dive onto the bank and thrust your face into the stream. It's the most refreshing drink of your life. But as soon as you feel replenished, your thoughts turn to Kate. You realize that you have no way of bringing the water back to her.

To make matters worse, you didn't note the direction from which you came. You see only trees and darkness.

You're lost. Your sister needs you, and you can't do anything about it.

"Kate!"

Does she hear you?

"Kate!"

Will she answer?

"Kate!"

*Can* she answer?

You collapse to the ground, sobbing.

There, you finally fall asleep.

**Turn to page 127.**

You decide to try a red berry. Red is good, right? Apples, cherries and strawberries are all red.

You bring the fruit to your mouth, but you hesitate. The more you think about eating it, the scarier the idea becomes. What if you get too sick to help your sister?

You tell yourself that you need to regain your strength. It's the best thing you can do for Kate right now. You take a deep, nervous breath and pop the fruit into your mouth. The burst of juice is a paradise of flavor. You celebrate your decision, feeling certain that you've made the right choice.

For ten minutes you gorge yourself on red berries, until at last you decide that you've had your fill. Your energy has returned, at least for now, and you feel strong enough to continue. Rejuvenated and ready, you fill your pockets with the tasty fruit. Then you start your journey anew, making sure that you break a tree branch every twenty steps.

**Turn to page 107.**

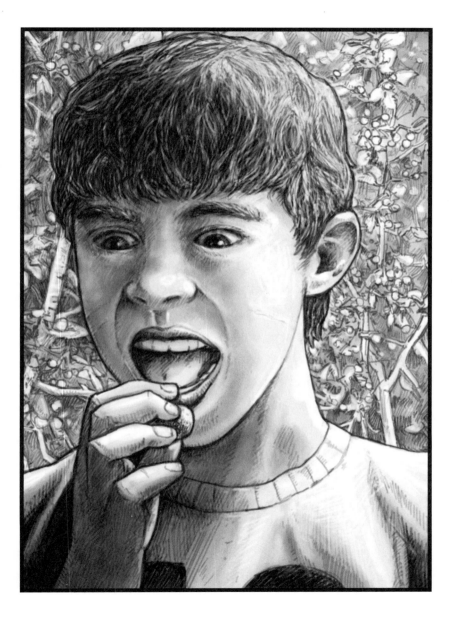

# 8
## WOLVES

The situation is almost too much. Your sister is lying behind you, unable to move. In front of you, at least seven wolves await their opportunity to pounce.

The largest of them steps closer. The others stay a few feet behind. They don't move until he does. He must be their leader. He'll probably be the first to attack.

You wish you could take a moment to consider how frightened you are. You wish you had time to catalog your many aches—from the empty rumble in your gut to the throbbing stabs in your arms and legs. But time is working against you. In moments the leader will charge, the others will follow, and then it will be too late.

How do you fend off seven wolves? How will you keep them away from your sister? Should you get them to chase you? Attack them first? Play dead?

You aren't sure, but Kate's life and yours may depend on this decision. What will you choose to do?

*If you run away, making as much noise as possible, you may trick the wolves into chasing you. It will ensure Kate's safety, and you'll have a better chance of escaping them.*

*Otherwise, instead of running, you can try scaring the wolves by going on the offensive. If you attack the leader, maybe he'll order his pack to retreat.*

*However, both of those decisions require action, and you may not have enough energy. Plus, either decision may provoke the wolves further. The best idea might be to play dead and hope they leave you alone.*

**If you choose to lead the wolves away from Kate, turn to page 21.**

**If you choose to attack the wolves, turn to page 60.**

**If you choose to play dead, turn to page 116.**

*HINT: If earlier in the story you chose to stay in your tent and read, turn to page 145 for a helpful hint.*

The hospital is surprisingly fun. Sure, you have needles and tubes sticking out of you—IV fluids for dehydration is what the doctor said. But you also have an almost endless supply of movies to watch. Plus there are video games, not to mention your cozy mattress and air conditioning!

The doctor hasn't let you eat yet. Again, it's that IV thing. But you're already planning your first meal: chicken strips, french fries and a chocolate chip cookie.

You almost start to drool, but your parents enter the room, ruining your fast-food fantasy.

They're crying.

"Jamie, there's something we have to tell you." Your dad chokes out the words. "Kate, she . . ."

"What?" you ask.

He sighs, heavily. "She didn't make it. They found her in the woods, but it was too late. If only they'd gotten to her a couple hours sooner . . ."

After that, your memories become hazy and blurred. You remember the next day. And the next. And the next. They meld together into weeks.

You remember the weeks becoming months.

You remember your mom and dad saying, time and again, that it isn't your fault. You don't believe it.

Memories are all you have left of your sister, but those memories are mixed with guilt. You're sure that, if you would've done things differently, she'd be alive today. You could've gotten her out of the forest. You could've helped her reach safety.

Instead, you chose poorly. It's a decision you'll regret for the rest of your life.

**Turn to page 139.**

You remember reading this rhyme in your survival book: "Berries white, poisonous sight."

**If you choose to eat mushrooms, turn to page 122.**
**If you choose to eat red berries, turn to page 68.**
**If you choose to eat white berries, turn to page 112.**

Whether mere minutes pass or several hours, you're not sure. But at last the forest begins to brighten. You can make out the trees' shapes and colors in every direction.

As Kate sleeps beside you, you consider a plan for the day. She needs a doctor, but she can't walk. She can't even stand. The two of you are deep in the woods, which makes you hard to find. It could be days or even weeks before anyone locates you. Given Kate's condition, you can't wait. You make a tough choice: You'll leave your sister behind, while you find help.

The idea of wandering alone in this deadly environment causes you to shudder. Worse than that, you dread the thought of Kate alone, helpless and vulnerable. But you remind yourself that you're doing this for her, and you commit to your decision.

Before you can leave, though, you have to make sure she's well enough to fend for herself. Her leg has swollen like an inner tube. That's not a good sign, but there's nothing you can do.

You take her hand, and it feels warmer than before. You check her pulse, and it has slowed as she slept. You gently brush her face, and her eyes open.

"Hi, Jamie," she says in a weary, morning voice.

"How are you feeling?" you ask.

She glares, as only a sibling can.

"Right," you mumble. "Dumb question."

Her eyes soften. "Yes, it's a dumb question. But thanks for caring."

Kate is in rough shape, but she's alert. She appears strong enough to survive on her own, at least for a while. That means you need to get moving. There's no time to waste.

"Kate, I have to leave," you say. "I have to get help."

She frowns, and you expect an argument. But your sister surprises you. She nods. "That's a dangerous choice, Jamie. But you can use the sun to find your way. Keep it on your left, and walk. You should reach the lake before noon. Are you sure you'll be okay by yourself?"

Kate's advice is meant to help. But in truth, it scares you. No, you're *not* sure if you'll be okay by yourself. In fact, during the night, you ran wildly without noting distance or direction. You see nothing but trees all around. You don't know which way you came or which way to go.

But to wait here, with Kate so badly injured, could also be a deadly decision.

What will you choose to do?

*Kate needs a doctor, and it could take weeks for anyone to find you in the middle of the forest. Her best chance is for you to bring help back to her.*

*However, you don't want to leave Kate behind. Both of you will be alone again, and that puts each of you in more danger, especially since she's injured. You're safer if you stay together.*

**If you choose to search for help, turn to page 96.**

**If you choose to stay with Kate, turn to page 137.**

*HINT: If earlier in the story you chose to swim with Kate, turn to page 52 for a helpful hint.*

After more than three hours of walking, you begin to lose hope. You should have found Kate by now. If not her, you should have reached shore. You're tired, you're hungry, and you want this nightmare to be over.

You force a path through cluster after cluster of trees. It's an exhausting process, but at last you push, past a final wave of leaves and branches, into a vast clearing.

The bright sun and cloudless sky blind you for a brief moment, and you don't immediately realize where you are. But then you see the beautiful, blue lake. Suddenly it makes sense. You've found your way out of the forest.

You rush into the cool water and splash around. Then, feeling as refreshed and as comfortable as possible, given the situation, you slump into the warm sand and wait.

**Turn to page 134.**

Without your map and compass, you aren't sure which way to go, but the sun provides a clue. You remember the sun rising on your right as you paddled to your fishing spot. So if you walk with the sun on your left, you should be moving back toward camp.

With this in mind, you decide to go left. You turn and begin your long hike to safety.

**Turn to page 31.**

You hear the boat before you see it. The thunderous rumble of its large motor echoes in the distance. The sound grows louder, and you allow yourself to hope that help is on the way.

When the vessel appears in the distance, you wave your arms and shout, praying that the crew will spot you. It turns in your direction and zooms forward, bringing with it an intense feeling of relief. You're about to be saved!

The boat stops a few feet offshore. Two men in ranger uniforms hop out and rush toward you.

You instantly become aware of your exhaustion. Every inch of your body throbs in pain. The agonizing sensation forces you onto your knees, and you let out a soft gasp, just before the rangers reach you.

"Jamie Manning?" one of them says. "Are you Jamie Manning?"

You nod as they help you back onto your feet, and then you blurt. " My sister, you have to help her!"

"Do you know where she is?" the same ranger asks. His voice sounds stern, but his eyes reveal an inner warmth and compassion.

"No," you tell him. "The storm. We fell out of our canoe. I haven't seen her since."

The ranger nods and begins to speak again, but he's interrupted by his partner. "We have Jamie's dad on the radio. He's on his way here."

**Turn to page 24.**

Your mother is there, waiting.

She grabs you. She squeezes you tightly, tears streaming down her face.

She holds you. She kisses you. She says she loves you. "Do you know where Kate is?" she asks.

"No," you tell her. "The storm. We fell out of the canoe. I haven't seen her since. I'm sorry, Mom. I'm sorry."

She hugs you again. "It's okay, honey. I love you, and you're safe."

The reunion is interrupted. A walkie-talkie squawks. Some ranger—or maybe a police officer—must have given it to your mother.

You hear your father's voice through the two-way radio. "Bonnie, are you there?"

Your mom quickly grabs it and presses a button. "I'm here, Jason. Jamie's with me."

"I'll be back as fast as I can," he says, and then the radio goes silent.

**Turn to page 24.**

Your survival instincts awaken. You tell yourself that Kate has already made it to land. You need to do the same.

You calm yourself. You take a deep breath. You close your eyes. In your mind, you try to picture what you saw before the storm. You try to remember which shoreline is nearest.

It doesn't help. You can't even tell which way you're facing. All you can see in every direction is water, rain and darkness.

You slowly and steadily begin kicking your legs. You propel yourself forward. Are you moving closer to land or farther from it? You wish you knew.

**Turn to page 64.**

Your fingers graze the weapon you need. You squeeze your hand around the pocketknife, pulling it out of your backpack. You feel a tinge of guilt as you aim your blade at the bear's snout. But your life is at stake. So is your sister's.

You jab the mama bear three times on her nose. The poor creature bellows in pain. She attacks again. She scratches your arm and bites your hand. You jab with your knife, again and again.

The bear retreats out of her den. She scurries away, disappearing from view.

Your hand is injured. You'll need medical attention soon. But for now, you're safe.

With the pocketknife in one hand and your backpack in the other, you slide out of the den. You take a quick look around.

Satisfied that the bear won't follow, you run.

**If you have a cell phone in your backpack, turn to page 115.**

**If you didn't bring a cell phone but have a compass in your backpack, turn to page 130.**

**If you packed neither, turn to page 123.**

The first and most important step to any survival situation is to stay calm. You remember reading that in your book. But right now, being calm isn't a problem. You're more than calm. You're bored. Of course, you also remember your book preaching patience. Don't make rash decisions, and don't second-guess your choices.

You're second-guessing this one. How long have you been waiting? Four hours? And how much longer will it be before Kate—or anyone—finds you?

You imagine your sister, somewhere along the shore, sitting in her own spot, wondering when you'll come. What if she's hurt? What if she has a concussion (or worse)?

As for your parents, maybe they think you went for a hike and the storm blew away the canoe. Maybe they're searching in all the wrong places.

It's time to move, time to do something. Or is it? What about the book's advice? You're not sure. You're hungry, tired and confused. You want your—

A terrible scream echoes through the forest, distracting you from your thoughts. It's Kate. She's far off, but it's her.

And there it is again: another scream. Your sister is alive, but something's wrong.

You jump to your feet and shout her name. She doesn't

answer. Instead, she screams a third time. You yell again. Still, she only screams.

You rush into the dense cluster of trees, shouting, "Kate!"

The branches extend toward you like a thousand arms reaching forward. Their edges are sharp. They scrape your hands, legs and face as you hurry past them. They're everywhere, all around you, never ending. You can't stop. You must find your sister. You have to make sure she's okay.

You fight through the thick vegetation, ignoring the pain and the blood. You weave around trees, over rocks and past bushes, following the sound of your sister's cries.

At last you break into a small clearing. A narrow stream flows gently down the middle of this open space. A bear cub laps up a drink of water with his long, pink tongue. Kate stands a few feet behind the cub, your backpack beside her. She must have grabbed it and brought it to shore.

For a moment, feelings of joy and relief return to you, but then you realize that Kate is crying. You see her take a deep, panicked breath, as if to scream yet again—and then you notice that Kate isn't looking at the cub.

She's staring at the cub's large, angry mother.

**Turn to page 88.**

# 5
# BEAR

You've never seen a bear before. This one has to be a black bear. It's the only type found in Minnesota. The animal is bigger than a refrigerator. Its teeth are the size of your thumb. You'd probably be excited if you weren't so scared. Kate is in real trouble.

You remember reading that black bears don't normally attack humans, but they might if they think their cubs are in danger. Kate is standing too close to that mama's baby. You know your sister would never hurt the cub. She loves animals, especially cute, harmless, little ones. But the black bear sees Kate as a threat.

The big bear glances at you and snarls. Kate shoots you a pleading look. The bear turns toward her again and roars.

Kate flinches. She takes a step backward.

She's going to run.

Is running away from a black bear the right thing to do? You scan your memory, trying to remember what you read about surviving a bear encounter. But your thoughts are like snakes, slithering away. You can't grab onto them. This is probably the most important moment of your life, and your brain isn't working. You're too panicked to think.

"Panic." The word sounds familiar. There was something in your book about panic. At last, you have an idea to cling to. Suddenly your memories come flooding back.

You step farther into the clearing. Part of you can't believe it. You're moving *toward* the bear. But it's the only way to help Kate.

"Jamie?" Her voice is breathless, tight. "What are you doing?" She gestures toward the large creature, as if you haven't seen it. "Get out of here! The bear!"

"Kate, listen to me. I'm going to tell you how to survive this situation."

What will you choose to tell her?

**If you'll tell Kate to run, turn to page 39.**
**If you'll tell her to back away slowly, turn to page 45.**
**If you'll tell her to climb a tree, turn to page 117.**

You dig into your backpack. You find nothing to fend off the bear. You use the only weapon you have: the bag. You desperately swing it against the animal's head, again and again. The beast ignores it.

The final moments of your life speed by too quickly. You see a flash of white teeth. You have time to regret some of the choices you've made. For an instant, you wonder what would've happened if you'd done things differently. Then everything goes black.

**Turn to page 139.**

You want to let Kate sleep, but you're afraid of what might be out there. Gently, you shake your sister. She slowly opens her eyes, confused and groggy.

To your right, the leaves rustle again.

"Do you hear that?" you whisper.

"Yes," she answers, sounding more than a little nervous. "What do you think it is?"

Kate hesitates. "I don't know."

A few feet away, something growls.

You hear soft, light footsteps. The sound moves closer.

Panic builds within you. It takes control. You want to cry. You want to scream. You want to get away.

Something brushes your hand. A leaf? A bug? A deadly creature? It doesn't matter. It's enough to get you onto your feet.

You violently tug Kate off the ground, almost pulling her arm out of socket. "Get up," you scream. "Run!"

You push her in front of you. She dashes into the nearest gathering of trees. You follow.

Your body is stiff with cold. The cuts and scrapes from yesterday sting and stretch. Everything hurts. You want to stop moving. But angry snarls are following you. Is it a bear? Something worse?

A loud "CRACK" fills the air, echoing through the night. It sounds as if a large branch has snapped in half. Kate lets out a piercing scream. She tumbles to the ground in front of you.

You stop in your tracks.

What happened? Where is she?

You crouch down, crawling toward the sound of her moans. "Kate," you whisper, as loudly as you dare. "Kate, where are you?"

"Jamie, my leg. It hurts!" Her words rise into a scream of anguish.

You fumble through the dirt and muck, until at last your hand brushes against her leg. She screams again.

"I'm sorry, but we have to move. Something's coming, and we never should've run. But now we have to move."

"I can't."

"I'll help." You grab her arm, pulling her off the ground. At first, she's able to push upward with her good leg. But then her injured leg shifts, and you hear the bones grind beneath her skin.

She shrieks and collapses, crying. "I can't, Jamie. It hurts, it hurts, it hurts."

You realize that you can't move your sister. It's too late

anyway. The animal has finally caught up. You hear it panting behind you. A low growling sound seems to come from everywhere.

You stand and turn, prepared to shield your sister from danger. When the animal attacks, you'll be ready.

But through the darkness, you make a startling discovery. There isn't one animal waiting to attack. There are several. You and your sister are almost entirely surrounded by a pack of wolves.

**Turn to page 70.**

After more than three hours of walking, you begin to lose hope. You should have found *something* by now. Where is the shore? You're tired, your body aches, and you want this nightmare to be over.

You force a path through cluster after cluster of trees. It's an exhausting process, but at last you push, past a final wave of leaves and branches, into a vast clearing.

The bright sun and cloudless sky blind you for a brief moment, and you don't immediately realize where you are. But then you see the beautiful, blue lake. Suddenly it makes sense. You've found your way out of the forest.

You rush into the cool water and splash around. Then, feeling as refreshed and as comfortable as possible, given the situation, you slump into the warm sand and wait.

**Turn to page 128.**

"I'll be fine," you assure her. "And I'll bring help as soon as I can."

You gather as many rocks and sticks as you can find, and you stack them beside her.

"If any animals get too close," you say, "throw a couple of these at them. It'll scare them off."

Your sister surprises you again, this time by pulling you into a gentle embrace. "I love you, Jamie."

"I love you too," you answer. Then you race away, so she won't see your tears.

**Turn to page 22.**

The direction you chose is the wrong one. You can see that now. You allow yourself another minute of rest before turning around and going back the way you came.

It's frustrating. You spent hours making good progress. Now you're returning to where you began. This hike has been a big waste of time and energy.

You try to recall your book's advice about wilderness survival. You remember reading that the most important step is to stay calm. But right now, being calm isn't a problem. You're more than calm. You're bored. Of course, you also remember your book preaching patience. Don't make rash decisions, and don't second-guess your choices.

You're second-guessing this one. How long have you been walking? Four hours? And how much longer will it be before you find Kate—or anyone?

You imagine your sister, somewhere along the shore, sitting in her own spot, wondering when you'll come. What if she's hurt? What if she has a concussion (or worse)?

As for your parents, by now they know you're missing. But maybe they think you went for a hike and the storm blew away the canoe. So maybe they're searching in all the wrong places.

You're hungry, tired and confused. You want your—

A terrible scream echoes through the forest, distracting you from your thoughts. It's Kate. She's far off, but it's her.

And there it is again: another scream. Your sister is alive, but something's wrong.

You shout her name. She doesn't answer. Instead, she screams a third time. You yell again. Still, she only screams.

You rush into the dense cluster of trees, shouting, "Kate!"

The branches extend toward you like a thousand arms reaching forward. Their edges are sharp. They scrape your hands, legs and face as you hurry past them. They're everywhere, all around you, never ending. You can't stop. You must find your sister. You have to make sure she's okay.

You fight through the thick vegetation, ignoring the pain and the blood. You weave around trees, over rocks and past bushes, following the sound of your sister's cries.

At last you break into a small clearing. A narrow stream flows gently down the middle of this open space, which is surrounded by trees. An adorable bear cub laps up a drink of water with his long, pink tongue. Kate stands just a few feet behind the cub, your blue backpack on the ground next to her. She must have grabbed it in the water and brought it to shore.

For a moment, feelings of joy and relief return to you,

but then you realize that Kate is crying. You see her take a deep, panicked breath, as if to scream yet again—and then you notice that Kate isn't looking at the cub.

She's staring at the cub's large, angry mother.

**Turn to page 88.**

# 4
## ALONE

You're awake. The sun has shifted. It must be afternoon.

You feel like you've fallen down a flight of stairs. Your head throbs, your body aches, and you aren't sure why. For the briefest moment, you forget where you are and what's happened. But it all comes back.

You lift your head, sending a ripple of pain down your spine. You remember Kate, lost in the wilderness, just like you are. You force the pain from your mind and push yourself up, out of the mud. You get onto your hands and knees. Then, with a soft grunt, you lift your hands off the ground and work your way onto your feet.

Your muscles burn like a newly lit match. Your empty stomach churns, begging for food. Your mouth tastes sandy and dry. But you won't allow yourself to think about your discomforts, not while Kate is missing.

You scan the lake's surface, and you suddenly realize it isn't raining any more. In fact, the sky is cloudless and blue. Under other circumstances, this would be a very pleasant morning. Now all you can do is wonder how long you've been asleep.

The lake is perfectly still, providing no trace of its earlier fury. There isn't a sign of Kate either—or the canoe, for that matter. You aren't sure whether that's good news or bad. The canoe has probably sunk (and your backpack along with it). But Kate was wearing a life jacket. If she were still in the water, you'd be able to see her. That means she must have reached shore too.

But where is she now? Is she searching for you? Or is she sitting somewhere, waiting for you to find her? For that matter, you can either wait for her to come upon you, or you can try to find her yourself.

What will you choose to do?

*If Kate is looking for you, she'll have a better chance of finding you if you stay in one place. If you leave your spot, you might walk in the wrong direction, away from her.*

*However, Kate could be waiting for you to find her. Or she might be injured. In that case, if you don't go looking for her, you may never reach her.*

If you choose to stay where you are, turn to page 53.
If you choose to look for Kate, turn to page 19.

*HINT: If earlier in the story you chose to swim with Kate, turn to page 142 for a helpful hint.*

# 7
## NIGHT

You know you should sleep. You're going to need your strength. But despite your best efforts, you can't seem to do it. Kate's arms are wrapped around you as she tries to keep you warm. It does little to brace you against the cold. Who could guess that such a hot day would be followed by this frigid night? You aren't sure what the temperature is, but you've never felt so cold before in your life.

You're miserable. You cannot imagine your situation getting worse—until you begin to hear noises. A twig snaps to your left. Leaves rustle to your right. You tell yourself it's nothing. Probably the wind. But you can't get yourself to believe it.

You're scared. You want to wake Kate. But she looks so peaceful. After today's trauma, you don't want to scare her without good reason.

What will you choose to do?

*Kate is tired. She needs her rest in order to regain her strength. Plus, if you hope to convince her to leave tomorrow, you don't want to scare her again.*

*However, danger could be lurking just a few feet away. If you don't awaken her now and if trouble does present itself, you may not have time to react.*

**If you choose to let Kate sleep, turn to page 59.**
**If you choose to awaken Kate, turn to page 91.**

Using the compass to stay on course, you force a path through cluster after cluster of trees. It's an exhausting process, but in less than two hours' time, you push past a final wave of leaves and branches, into a vast clearing.

The bright sun and the cloudless sky blind you for a moment. You don't immediately realize where you are. But then you see the beautiful, blue lake, and suddenly it makes sense. You've found your way out of the forest.

**If you brought waterproof matches in your backpack, turn to page 131.**

**If you don't have waterproof matches in your backpack, turn to page 140.**

As you march through the forest, your next discovery stops you mid-step. Up ahead, you spy a bear and her cub sitting outside a small den, dug into the hillside.

You peer toward the animals, afraid to move. You suddenly realize they're the same bears that you and Kate encountered less than twenty-four hours ago. You're certain of this fact, not because you recognize the mama bear or the playful cub, but because you can see directly into their den. And deep within it, you spot your blue backpack.

You want your bag, but you don't want to deal with those bears again. What will you choose to do?

*Venturing into a bear's den is a dangerous plan. If anything happens to you, Kate will never be found.*

*However, there are supplies inside your backpack, and you might need them to ensure your rescue. If you wait until the bears leave, you can minimize the danger . . . maybe.*

**If you choose to retrieve your bag, turn to page 54.**
**If you choose to continue walking, turn to page 95.**

Your search is a disaster. It takes more than an hour of wandering before you come across a small creek, trickling through the woods.

You dive onto the bank and thrust your face into the stream. It's the most refreshing drink of your life. But as soon as you feel replenished, your thoughts turn to Kate. You have no way of bringing the water back to her.

To make matters worse, you didn't note the direction from which you came. You see only trees all around you. You're lost.

"Kate!"

Does she hear you?

"Kate!"

Will she answer?

"Kate!"

Where is she?

Nowhere. Gone.

It appears you'll have to make your way out of this forest after all.

**Turn to page 22.**

The hospital is surprisingly fun. Sure, you have needles and tubes sticking out of you—IV fluids for dehydration is what the doctor said. But you also have an almost endless supply of movies to watch. Plus there are video games, not to mention a cozy mattress and air conditioning!

The doctor hasn't let you eat yet. Again, it's something about those IV fluids. But you're already planning your first meal: chicken strips, french fries and strawberry ice cream.

You almost start drooling, but your parents enter the room, ruining your fast-food fantasy.

They're forgiven. They brought a surprise visitor: Kate.

You can't remember a happier moment in your life. Your sister is in a wheelchair, with a huge white cast on her leg, and she has an IV thing too. But otherwise, she looks fine.

The doctor told you to stay in bed, but you can't hide your excitement. You leap from under the covers, an instant reminder of your many cuts and bruises. You grimace in pain but quickly hide it with a smile.

You skip forward, only to be stopped by the tug of your IV tube. This isn't how you imagined your reunion.

Kate simply laughs.

Your mom comes to the rescue, rolling your IV bag next to Kate's.

You try it again.

This time, you skip all the way to your sibling. You wrap your arms around her and squeeze tightly.

"You did it," she whispers. "You really did it. Thank you for saving my life."

You blush, unsure how to respond. "I'm sorry your leg got broken."

Kate smiles. "Don't worry. It'll be better in no time."

"Good," you say, "because as soon as it is, I want to go camping again."

Your statement surprises you almost as much as it does her. You didn't realize until this moment that the idea of staying in the woods, with all of its wild animals and other dangers, doesn't sound so scary any more. In fact, it sounds kind of fun. You've survived the worst that the forest has to offer, and you can't wait to do it again.

**Turn to page 111.**

# The End

**You survived
being
*LOST IN THE WILD!***

You decide to try a white berry. White is good, right?

You pick the fruit and bring it to your mouth. You hesitate. The more you think about eating it, the scarier the idea becomes. You're hungry. You desperately want food. But you're afraid of becoming too sick to help your sister.

You need to regain your strength. This is the best thing you can do for Kate right now. You take a deep, nervous breath, and you pop the fruit into your mouth.

The flavor is bitter and sour, but you force yourself to swallow it down.

You eat another. You begin to eat yet another. All of a sudden your stomach burns. The pain is intense, like a hundred needles pricking your insides.

It's unbearable. You fold over, clenching your gut. You fall to the ground.

You let out a wild scream of agony, and you ask yourself a haunting question: What would've happened if you made a different choice?

Sadly, you will never know.

**Turn to page 139.**

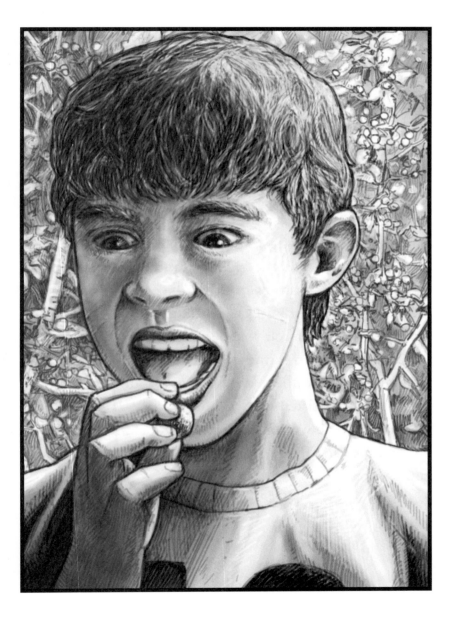

As you sit on the beach waiting, you hear the boat before you see it. The thunderous rumble of its large motor echoes in the distance. The sound grows louder, and you allow yourself to hope that help is on the way.

When the vessel appears in the distance, you wave your arms and shout, praying that the crew will spot you. It turns in your direction and zooms forward, bringing with it an intense feeling of relief. You're about to be saved!

The boat stops a few feet offshore. Two men in ranger uniforms hop out and rush toward you.

You instantly become aware of your exhaustion. Every inch of your body throbs in pain. The agonizing sensation forces you onto your knees, and you let out a soft gasp, just before the rangers reach you.

"Are you Jamie Manning?" one of them says.

You nod as they help you back onto your feet, and then you blurt. " My sister, you have to help her!"

"Do you know where she is?" the same ranger asks. His voice sounds stern, but his eyes reveal an inner warmth and compassion.

"Yes," you say. "She's in the forest. I'll take you to her."

**Turn to page 10.**

You pull your cell phone out of the backpack, ready to dial 9-1-1. You shake with excitement as you imagine the end of your troubles.

You press the power button. Water leaks out the side.

Your phone doesn't work. It was ruined by lake water when your canoe capsized.

**If you have a compass, turn to page 130.**

**If you don't have a compass, turn to page 123.**

Some people have survived animal attacks by playing dead. That was in your book. But will it work against a pack of wolves? You're not sure, but it's your best option.

You dive onto the ground. You whisper to Kate, "Don't move. Don't make a sound."

Despite her injury, she does as you tell her. The two of you share an uneasy silence.

Minutes pass.

Has your plan worked?

A wolf pounces on top of you, followed by another and then another.

You hear snarls and growls. You're helpless.

You see a flash of white teeth. You wonder what would've happened if you'd made a different choice. Then everything goes black.

**Turn to page 139.**

"Climb a tree," you tell her. "Go!"

She turns and dashes toward the forest. She leaps into the nearest tree, climbing as quickly as she can.

Kate's fast. The animal is faster. Four bounds and the bear is to the tree. It climbs after her. *Black bears can climb!*

The beast bites your sister's leg, pulling her to the ground with a thud.

Kate screams. You rush to her aid. It's the last mistake you ever make.

The mama bear turns toward you. She lunges with a snarl. You see a flash of white teeth.

You have a moment to wonder what would've happened if you made a different choice. Then everything goes black.

**Turn to page 139.**

# 9
## SHOCK

When it comes to treating shock, little things can make a big difference. You learned that, too. You immediately begin talking in your calmest voice. "Kate, it's me, Jamie. I'm here. I'm going to help." You slowly roll her onto her back, taking special care not to jostle her wounded leg.

"There you go," you whisper. "How do you feel?"

She begins to cry. "I'm cold. I'm so cold."

"I'll do my best to keep you warm, Kate. But first I need to make sure you're nice and comfortable, okay?"

She doesn't answer.

You gently lift her into a sitting position. You prop her against a tree.

"I feel dizzy," she tells you.

"Don't worry, Kate. I think that's normal."

She closes her eyes. Her face looks ghostly pale. She needs water. So do you.

"Sit still and relax," you whisper. "This is *definitely* an emergency. I'm going to find some water."

With that, you quietly stand, turn and begin your search for something to drink.

**Turn to page 67.**

It scares you to sleep out in the open, but it scares you even more to leave Kate behind. For her sake and yours, you'll wait. Maybe she'll change her mind.

Unfortunately, the evening grows dark quickly. You can't make your way back to the lake now, even if Kate decides to do so. If you and your sister had gone back right away, a passing boat might have spotted you. But now the two of you will have to sleep by yourselves, without food, shelter or adults.

Kate has the same thought. "They're not going to find us tonight. Do you know how to make a fire?"

You shake your head. "Not without my book."

"Then we should build ourselves a bed," she tells you.

The setting sun steals the air's warmth, and you begin to shiver. But at least the hot day has managed to dry your clothes, for the most part.

The pain in your gut reminds you that you haven't eaten since sunrise. You long for your backpack. There's food in your bag. But, of course, that's probably why the mama bear took it. More than that, though, there are items inside the backpack that could help you. You wish you had them, but wishing doesn't do any good. If you're going to survive, you'll need to make use of whatever you can find.

You're thirsty. You want to drink from the stream, but Kate stops you. Something about intestinal parasites and boiling water and don't drink unless it's an emergency.

She asks you to gather all of the leaves and grass you can carry. It sounds easy, but it isn't. You have to dig deep under bushes and fallen trees to find anything that isn't damp.

In the meantime, she picks more than thirty large rocks from along the stream's bank. She uses them to form a circle on the ground, one that's big enough to lie in, and then she begins piling the leaves and grass inside. It's a good idea. The circle of rocks should keep most of the materials from scattering. They should offer *some* protection against the cold forest floor.

You help Kate build a tall mound and spread it evenly within the circle of rocks. You wish you had your life jacket. That extra padding would definitely help. Kate's not wearing her life jacket either. She must've left it behind, too.

When the last of the day's light disappears, you and your sister lie on your makeshift bed. It provides only a bit of comfort against the chilly, dark night. But you hold each other tightly, and that—at least—is something.

**Turn to page 104.**

You decide to try a mushroom. Mushrooms are safe, right? People eat mushrooms on pizza, hamburgers and any number of foods.

You bring the fungi to your mouth, but you hesitate. The more you think about eating it, the scarier the idea becomes. What if you get too sick to help your sister?

You tell yourself that you need to regain your strength. It's the best thing you can do for Kate right now. You take a deep, nervous breath and pop the mushroom into your mouth. The flavor is bland. You force yourself to swallow it.

You eat another. You begin to eat yet another. All of a sudden your stomach burns. The pain is intense, like a hundred needles pricking your insides.

It's unbearable. You fold over, clenching your gut. You fall to the ground.

You let out a wild scream of agony, and you ask yourself a haunting question: What would've happened if you made a different choice?

Sadly, you will never know.

**Turn to page 139.**

# 12
## SHORE

Safely away from the bear, you take out your map. You try to decide where you are and which way to go. Without a compass, it's impossible. In the end, you're forced to guess which direction to walk.

After your frightful encounter with the bear, you feel weak and more than a little shaken. You allow yourself a few minutes' rest, using the chance to snack on a pocketful of berries.

Your energy returns too slowly. You're almost too tired to stand. But thoughts of your sister propel you to action. You breathe a deep, weary sigh and continue on your way.

**Turn to page 25.**

You hear the helicopter before you see it. The thunderous THUM-THUM-THUM of its large propeller echoes in the distance. Gradually, the sound grows louder. You allow yourself to hope that help is on the way. When the aircraft appears in the distant sky, you wave your arms and shout, praying that the crew will spot you.

The helicopter turns in your direction and zooms forward, bringing with it an intense feeling of relief. You're about to be rescued. Soon the chopper is hovering above your signal fire, and then it slowly descends onto a nearby beach. Two men in ranger uniforms hop out and rush toward you.

You instantly become aware of your exhaustion. Every inch of your body throbs with pain. The agonizing sensation forces you onto your knees. You gasp softly, just before the rangers reach you.

"Jamie Manning," one of them says. "Are you Jamie Manning?"

You nod as they help you back onto your feet. " My sister! You have to help her!"

"Do you know where she is?" the same ranger asks. His voice sounds stern, but his eyes reveal an inner warmth and compassion.

You offer your map to the two rescuers, and you point to the area where Kate might be. The gesture is small, but it steals your remaining energy. "She's there, somewhere. I think she has a broken leg."

The rangers smile at you and promise to look for her. It's the last thing you remember before passing out.

**Turn to page 109.**

Whether mere minutes pass or several hours, you're not sure. But at last the forest begins to brighten. You can make out the trees' shapes and colors in every direction.

You consider a plan for the day. Kate is out there somewhere. You either have to find your sister or find someone else who can.

Without knowing where you are or where she is, you do the only thing you can. You walk.

**Turn to page 78.**

You hear the boat before you see it. The thunderous rumble of its large motor echoes in the distance. Gradually, the sound grows louder, and you allow yourself to hope that help is on the way. When the vessel appears in the distance, you wave your arms and shout, praying that the crew will spot you.

It turns in your direction and zooms forward, bringing with it an intense feeling of relief: You're about to be saved. The boat stops just a few feet offshore, and then two men in ranger uniforms hop out and rush toward you.

You instantly become aware of your exhaustion. Every inch of your body throbs in pain. The agonizing sensation forces you onto your knees, and you let out a soft gasp just before the rangers reach you.

"Jamie Manning," one of them says. "Are you Jamie Manning?"

You nod as they help you back onto your feet, and then you blurt. "My sister, you have to help her!"

"Do you know where she is?" the same ranger asks. His voice sounds stern, but his eyes reveal an inner warmth and compassion.

"She's in the forest," you tell him. "I marked a trail by breaking tree branches."

"It'll be hard to follow a trail like that," admits the ranger. "Plenty of branches get broken in the forest. If you point us in the right direction, we'll do our best to find her."

The ranger smiles and begins to speak again, but he is interrupted by his partner. "We have Jamie's dad on the radio. He's on his way here."

They're the last words you remember hearing before you pass out.

**Turn to page 109.**

# 12
## SHORE

Safely away from the bear, you take out your map and compass. You find the spot that represents the clearing and the stream—the place where you first found your sister.

From there, you can figure out where you swam to shore. You can even guess where you left Kate behind. More importantly, you know which way to go. The lake is south, and it isn't far. But to get there quickly, you'll need to veer slightly to your right.

After your frightful encounter with the mama bear, you feel weak and more than a little shaken. You allow yourself a few minutes' rest, using the opportunity to snack on a pocketful of berries.

Your energy returns too slowly. You're almost too tired to stand. But thoughts of your sister propel you to action. You breathe a deep, weary sigh and continue on your way.

**Turn to page 106.**

You fantasize about rushing into the cool water or even slumping into the warm sand, but your work isn't finished. You turn around and march back into the woods, gathering every dry twig and small branch you can uncover.

You pull *Survival Kids* out of your backpack. Carefully following the book's instructions, you begin to build a signal fire—step by step.

You use your waterproof matches to light the smallest twigs, as well as a few blank pages at the end of your book, on fire. You add the bigger logs, allowing the flame to grow. And finally, you almost smother the fire with green leaves and moss, creating a thick upward flow of white smoke. It isn't the fire that will lead rescuers to you. It's the smoke.

You're pleased with yourself for creating such a strong signal, but you can't rest yet. Your job is now to keep the fire burning and the signal alive. Instead of sitting down, as you desperately wish to do, you trudge back into the forest to gather another load of supplies.

**Turn to page 124.**

# 9
## SHOCK

When it comes to treating shock, little things can make a big difference. You learned that, too. You immediately begin talking in your calmest voice. "Kate, it's me, Jamie. I'm here. I'm going to help." You slowly roll her onto her back, taking special care not to jostle her wounded leg. You create a small pillow of dirt under her head, just enough to help her rest.

"There you go," you whisper. "How do you feel?"

She begins to cry. "I'm cold. I'm so cold."

"I'll do my best to keep you warm, Kate. But first I need to make sure you're nice and comfortable, okay?"

She doesn't answer, so you continue working. You recall being taught that you're supposed to loosen a shock victim's clothing. You untie her boots and unbuckle her belt.

Next, you must raise Kate's legs, but your instincts tell you not to reposition her injury. You compromise. You leave her wounded leg alone, but you lift her good leg about ten inches off the ground. You build a pile of sticks, dirt and grass beneath and gently rest her leg on top of the mound.

Having done all you can for your sister, you quickly find your hiking boots. As you put them on, you silently thank your dad for buying such a sturdy pair.

Then finally, you snuggle beside Kate. It's your turn to share the warmth that your body can offer. You tell her to be strong, as you helplessly wait in the darkness.

Morning cannot come soon enough.

**Turn to page 75.**

You hear the boat before you see it. The thunderous rumble of its large motor echoes in the distance. The sound grows louder, and you allow yourself to hope that help is on the way.

When the vessel appears in the distance, you wave your arms and shout, praying that the crew will spot you. It turns in your direction and zooms forward, bringing with it an intense feeling of relief. You're about to be saved!

The boat stops a few feet offshore. Two men in ranger uniforms hop out and rush toward you.

You instantly become aware of your exhaustion. Every inch of your body throbs in pain. The agonizing sensation forces you onto your knees, and you let out a soft gasp, just before the rangers reach you.

"Jamie Manning?" one of them says. "Are you Jamie Manning?"

You nod as they help you back onto your feet, and then you blurt. " My sister, you have to help her!"

"Do you know where she is?" the same ranger asks. His voice sounds stern, but his eyes reveal an inner warmth and compassion.

"No," you tell him. "I lost her in the forest. I haven't seen her since."

The ranger nods and begins to speak again, but he is interrupted by his partner. "We have Jamie's dad on the radio. He's on his way here."

**Turn to page 24.**

Your fingers graze the weapon you need. You squeeze your hand around the pepper spray, pulling it out of your backpack. You feel a tinge of guilt as you aim at the bear's snout. After all, the animal is simply defending her home. But your life is at stake, and so is your sister's.

The den is dark, but your finger atop the canister tells you it's aimed in the right direction. You press the button. It hisses, releasing a vile spray directly into the animal's mouth and nose. The poor creature releases your boot and bellows her disapproval. The bear backs out of the den and rolls onto the ground, pawing at her face.

With the pepper spray in one hand and your backpack in the other, you scurry out of the cave. You're ready to blast the mama bear again, but the animal remains on the ground, rolling and sweeping her face. The bear will recover soon enough, but right now she poses no threat.

Satisfied that the beast will not follow, you run.

**If you have a cell phone in your backpack, turn to page 115.**

**If you didn't bring a cell phone but have a compass in your backpack, turn to page 130.**

**If you packed neither, turn to page 123.**

"It's probably best for us to stay together," you say. "I'll wait here with you."

The look on her face tells you how relieved she is. Kate doesn't want to be alone any more than you do, but you wonder whether it's the right choice.

"Are you thirsty?" she asks, changing the subject.

"Yes, and I'm hungry too," you admit.

"Do you think you can maybe find something for us to drink—and eat? We might be here a while. We're going to need food and water."

"I thought we weren't supposed to drink the water," you remind your sister. "It isn't safe."

"You can in an emergency. This *definitely* qualifies."

"Okay, I'll have a look around." With that said, you turn and leave.

**Turn to page 108.**

# The End

## Try again

You hear the boat before you see it. The thunderous rumble of its large motor echoes in the distance. Gradually, the sound grows louder, and you allow yourself to hope that help is on the way. When the vessel appears in the distance, you wave your arms and shout, praying that the crew will spot you.

It turns in your direction and zooms forward, bringing with it an intense feeling of relief: You're about to be saved. The boat stops just a few feet offshore, and then two men in ranger uniforms hop out and rush toward you.

You instantly become aware of your exhaustion. Every inch of your body throbs in pain. The agonizing sensation forces you onto your knees, and you let out a soft gasp just before the rangers reach you.

"Jamie Manning," one of them says. "Are you Jamie Manning?"

You nod as they help you back onto your feet, and then you blurt. " My sister, you have to help her!"

"Do you know where she is?" the same ranger asks. His voice sounds stern, but his eyes reveal an inner warmth and compassion.

"She's in the forest," you tell him. "I marked a trail by breaking tree branches."

"It'll be hard to follow a trail like that," admits the ranger. "Plenty of branches get broken in the forest. If you point us in the right direction, we'll do our best to find her."

The ranger smiles and begins to speak again, but he is interrupted by his partner. "We have Jamie's dad on the radio. He's on his way here."

They're the last words you remember hearing before you pass out.

**Turn to page 72.**

Knowing Kate, she's already looking for you. By waiting where you are, you'll have a better chance of being found.

**If you choose to stay where you are, turn to page 53.**
**If you choose to look for Kate, turn to page 19.**

As you decide what to do, you recall a rhyme Kate taught you. "If the face is red, lift the head. If the face is pale, lift the tail."

Kate's face is definitely pale.

**If you choose to elevate her uninjured leg and keep her warm, turn to page 132.**

**If you choose to elevate her head and find her a drink of water, turn to page 118.**

Some bears have been known to watch from a distance, even after they leave an area. If you follow the bear, she might attack again.

**If you choose to return to the lake, turn to page 20.**
**If you choose to search for your backpack, turn to page 44.**

Your book told you that wolves often chase their prey. However, they prefer to target sick, injured or dead animals because they're easier to catch.

**If you choose to lead the wolves away from Kate, turn to page 21.**

**If you choose to attack the wolves, turn to page 60.**

**If you choose to play dead, turn to page 116.**

*Choose four of the following items. Mark your choices, so you remember what's in your backpack. But be careful: The items you select might mean the difference between life and death.*

**Bottled water:** When it comes to survival needs, water is at the top of the list. Bring this to ensure that you do not get dehydrated, making you too weak to carry on.

**Cell phone:** Reception is very poor in the Boundary Waters. But if you get into trouble, it'll be nice to know that help is just a phone call away.

**Compass:** This is the only item that can ensure you don't get lost. You'll always know which direction you're going, as long as you have your compass.

**First-aid kit:** Cuts and wounds are common, but they can get infected and become life-threatening. Treating them with a first-aid kit is the only way to ensure that doesn't happen.

**Mosquito repellent:** You already know that mosquito bites can make you sick. This item is guaranteed to keep mosquitoes (and other bugs) away.

**Pepper spray:** Defend yourself against animal attacks. Spray this into an animal's face, and the critter will run off.

**Pocketknife:** This handy trinket is for cleaning fish, cutting small branches and countless other uses. Most outdoorsmen never leave home without their trusty pocketknife.

**Rope:** You never know when you'll need this. It's ideal for tying a shelter together, pulling someone out of a deep hole or making a raft.

**Waterproof matches:** If you need to start a fire, you'll want these. After all, creating flame by rubbing sticks together isn't as easy as it sounds.

**Whistle:** Make yourself easy to find. If you ever get separated from your family, blow this whistle. The sound will lead them to you.

**After you've made your choices, turn to page 26.**

# CAMPING SAFETY TIPS

- Bring an adult with you.

- Pack enough food, clothing and equipment to keep you safe and comfortable in case of emergency.

- Always tell someone at home where you're going and when you'll be back.

- Plan to arrive at your campsite with more than enough daylight to set up camp.

- Build your campfire in an open area, away from bushes, trees and especially branches that might extend over the flame. Always make sure someone is watching the fire, and keep a large bucket of water nearby.

- If you leave your campsite, return before dark.

- Check weather forecasts before you go. Keep an eye on weather conditions while you're camping.

- When exploring, stay on the trails.

- Plan a place to meet, in case someone in your group gets separated from the others.

- Take a first-aid and outdoor safety course.

# OUTDOOR SURVIVAL TIPS

- Bring an adult with you.
- Plan for the unexpected. Pack food and water, matches, pepper spray, a pocketknife, a first-aid kit, a map and compass, an emergency signaling device, and anything else you might need.
- Always tell someone at home where you're going and when you'll be back.
- Plan safe activities that won't take more skill or energy than you have.
- Wear a hat (in hot weather and in cold).
- If you're lost, stop moving. Stay in one place. Stay calm, and think of ways to signal for help.
- When hiking through bear country, make plenty of noise. For instance, you can wear a bell, blow a whistle or shout regularly.
- If possible, keep your clothes dry.
- Assume all wild fruits and mushrooms are poisonous.
- Take a first-aid and outdoor safety course.

# DON'T BE SCARED OF . . .

## BLACK BEARS

- Black Bears almost never attack humans, even if their cubs are nearby.

- Most Black Bears are afraid of humans, so the best way to prevent an attack is to make lots of noise.

- Never approach or try to touch a Black Bear, and never crawl into a Black Bear's den.

## GRAY WOLVES

- Most Gray Wolves are afraid of humans. In fact, wolf attacks on humans are very rare in North America.

- Gray Wolves will usually go out of their way to avoid humans.

- If you never feed, approach or try to touch a Gray Wolf, you will probably never be attacked by one.

# REFERENCES

*Camping Safety Tips.* www.familycampinggear.com/generic22.html. Family Camping Gear, 2001–2008.

*Gray Wolf (canis lupus).* www.fws.gov/midwest/wolf/biology/biologue.htm. U.S. Fish and Wildlife Service: Midwest Region. 2007.

*Health and Safety Tips: Hiking and Camping Safety.* www.redcross.org/services/hss/tips/hiking.html. American Red Cross. 2008.

*Ron Cordes Pocket Guide to Outdoor Survival, The.* Ron Cordes and Stan Bradshaw. Pocket Guides Publishing, Inc., Santa Rosa, CA. 2005.

*Shape Safety Bulletin #31A: British Columbia Wildlife.* www.shape.bc.ca/resources/bulletins/31a-BCwildlife.pdf. Safety and Health in Arts Production and Entertainment, Vancouver. 2006.

*Things That Bite: A Realistic Look at Critters That Scare People.* Tom Anderson. Adventure Publications, Inc., Cambridge, MN. 2008.

*Worst-Case Scenario Almanac: Great Outdoors, The.* David Borgenict and Trey Popp. Chronicle Books, San Francisco. 2007.

# ABOUT THE AUTHOR

Ryan Jacobson has always loved choose-your-path books, so he was thrilled to get a chance to write one. He used his memories of those fun-filled stories and his past experiences as a camp counselor (a highlight of which included a five-day, fifty-two-mile canoe trip), to write *Lost in the Wild*.

Ryan is the author of eight children's books, including a picture book, three comic books, three chapter books and a choose-your-path book. He lives in Mora, Minnesota, with his wife Lora, son Jonah and dog Boo.

For more about Ryan, visit RyanJacobsonOnline.com.